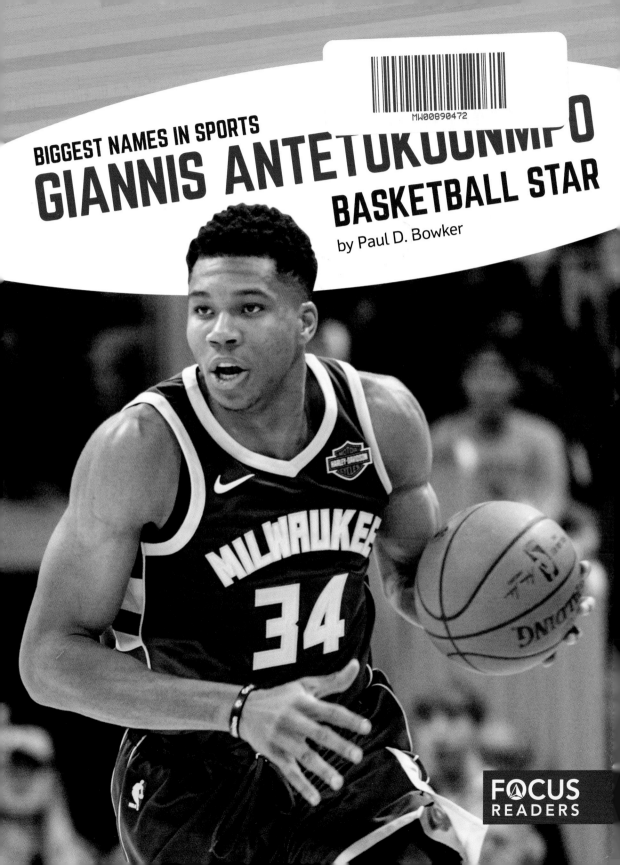

BIGGEST NAMES IN SPORTS
GIANNIS ANTETOKOUNMPO
BASKETBALL STAR

by Paul D. Bowker

FOCUS READERS

WWW.FOCUSREADERS.COM

Focus Readers is distributed by North Star Editions:
sales@northstareditions.com | 888-417-0195

Produced for Focus Readers by Red Line Editorial.

Photographs ©: John Amis/AP Images, cover, 1; Tom Lynn/AP Images, 4–5, 7, 9; AP Images, 10–11; Elias Verdi/Alamy, 12; Morry Gash/AP Images, 15; Nick Wass/AP Images, 16–17; Tony Dejak/AP Images, 19; John Fisher/Cal Sport Media/AP Images, 21; Nathan Denette/ The Canadian Press/AP Images, 22–23, 25; Phelan M. Ebenhack/AP Images, 27; Red Line Editorial, 29

ISBN
978-1-63517-866-1 (hardcover)
978-1-63517-967-5 (paperback)
978-1-64185-170-1 (ebook pdf)
978-1-64185-069-8 (hosted ebook)

Library of Congress Control Number: 2018931670

Printed in the United States of America
Mankato, MN
May, 2018

ABOUT THE AUTHOR

Paul D. Bowker is an editor and author who lives on Cape Cod in South Yarmouth, Massachusetts. His 35-year newspaper career has included hundreds of NBA games. He is a national past president of Associated Press Sports Editors and has won multiple national writing awards.

TABLE OF CONTENTS

CHAPTER 1

The Game Changer 5

CHAPTER 2

Growing Up in Greece 11

CHAPTER 3

The Rookie Rises 17

CHAPTER 4

Becoming a Superstar 23

At-a-Glance Map • 28
Focus on Giannis Antetokounmpo • 30
Glossary • 31
To Learn More • 32
Index • 32

THE GAME CHANGER

Giannis Antetokounmpo was playing for his father. It was that simple on the night of October 21, 2017.

Antetokounmpo had recently lost his dad to an unexpected heart attack. The memory of his father weighed heavily on his mind as the Milwaukee Bucks took on the Portland Trail Blazers.

Antetokounmpo pumps his fist after making a big basket against the Trail Blazers.

The Bucks were down by one point with only 31 seconds left in the game. Antetokounmpo had already scored 42 points. It was a career-best night for him. Now he stood at the free-throw line with the chance to put his team in the lead. But he missed his first shot. Then he missed his second.

Antetokounmpo refused to let it end that way. In the game's final 30 seconds, he took control. First, he stripped the ball away from Blazers guard C. J. McCollum. Then he outraced three Portland defenders and swooped in for a slam dunk. The Bucks were up by one point with 11 seconds left.

Antetokounmpo takes the ball to the hoop during a 2017 game against the Trail Blazers.

The Blazers had one last chance to win the game. One of their players drove to the basket. But Antetokounmpo met him there with a monster block to finish off his amazing night. The Bucks tacked on two free throws in the final seconds and won the game 113–110.

When Antetokounmpo made his way back to the locker room, he received a surprise. His teammates greeted him with the game ball. Antetokounmpo wrote a message on the ball. It said, "This is for Daddy. We got a win tonight, and I got 44 points."

THE GREEK FREAK

Because of his size and skill, Antetokounmpo is known as the Greek Freak. And he wears the name proudly. In fact, it didn't take long for Antetokounmpo to become a fan favorite in Milwaukee. That was especially true for the 10,000 people of Greek heritage who live in the city. Bucks fans have even made Antetokounmpo's jersey one of the league's top sellers.

Antetokounmpo's teammates congratulate him after his amazing game against the Trail Blazers.

Antetokounmpo knew his father would have been proud. The young Bucks star had come a long way from his humble beginnings in Greece.

CHAPTER 2

GROWING UP IN GREECE

Giannis Antetokounmpo was born on December 6, 1994. He grew up in a poor neighborhood in Athens, Greece. His mother and father had moved there from Lagos, Nigeria, in 1991. They hoped to build better lives in Greece.

Both of Giannis's parents were athletes. His dad had played soccer in Nigeria.

Giannis Antetokounmpo takes part in a training session with the Greek team Filathlitikos.

In the neighborhood where Giannis grew up, there is now a picture of him on a local basketball court.

His mom had been a high jumper. But in Greece, the family's main concern was finding work. Giannis and his older brother Thanasis often sold sunglasses and watches on the street. It was the only way they could earn money for food.

Giannis and Thanasis began to play basketball together in 2003. Giannis was just nine years old at the time. Basketball was a great way to forget about the family's struggles for a little while.

A DIFFICULT START

The Antetokounmpo family had a tough time when they first arrived in Greece. Earning enough money for food was often a challenge. That meant there wasn't much money left over for other things. Giannis had to share a bed with three brothers. Even today, Giannis often thinks back to that time. It makes him grateful for his success in the NBA.

One day, a coach spotted the brothers playing. The coach was from Filathlitikos, a local basketball team. He noticed the size of the two brothers and invited them to join the team.

Before long, Giannis had become the star of the team. He was already 6 feet 9 inches (206 cm) tall. He weighed 196 pounds (89 kg). And his **wingspan** was 7 feet 3 inches (221 cm).

He had the size. But he lacked the experience. Most **scouts** doubted that Antetokounmpo could succeed in the National Basketball Association (NBA). After all, he played in Greek leagues against teams that weren't very good.

Bucks general manager John Hammond introduces Antetokounmpo at a news conference in 2013.

But Milwaukee Bucks general manager John Hammond saw something the others did not. He watched Antetokounmpo play for three days in Greece. He decided the Bucks would choose Antetokounmpo with their first pick in the 2013 NBA **Draft**.

CHAPTER 3

THE ROOKIE RISES

Giannis Antetokounmpo was only 18 years old when the Milwaukee Bucks selected him. That made him the youngest player in the draft. Now that Antetokounmpo was in the NBA, his days of struggling for money were over. In his **rookie** season, he earned more than $1.7 million.

Antetokounmpo dunks the ball during his rookie season.

Antetokounmpo put his money to good use. He had a very close relationship with his family. So he paid for them to move to Milwaukee with him. He and his parents lived on separate floors in an apartment building. His mom and dad could finally enjoy **luxuries** they had not been able to afford in Nigeria or Greece.

Antetokounmpo had never played basketball at an American high school or college. But it didn't take him long to make his mark in the NBA. He had an impressive 61 blocks during the 2013–14 season. That was more than any other rookie in the league. People were starting to take notice.

Antetokounmpo tries to dribble past a defender during a 2013 game against the Cleveland Cavaliers.

But Antetokounmpo was the only bright spot for the Bucks that season. They finished the year with the worst record in the NBA.

Antetokounmpo continued to develop his skills during the off-season. He joined other young players in the NBA Summer League in 2014. Then he traveled to Europe to play with the Greek national basketball team.

During his second season with the Bucks, Antetokounmpo was even

GROWING AND GROWING

Antetokounmpo's height was 6 feet 9 inches (206 cm) when the Bucks drafted him in 2013. But he was not done growing yet. He added another 2 inches (5.1 cm) during his rookie season of 2013–14. He also put on weight. That meant Antetokounmpo had the right body to play power forward. He had been a point guard in Greece.

Antetokounmpo leaps toward the basket during a 2015 game against the Phoenix Suns.

better. His shooting improved, and he had more **rebounds**. Best of all, the Bucks were a much better team. They reached the **playoffs** for the first time in Antetokounmpo's career. The season ended in a first-round loss to the Chicago Bulls. Even so, fans in Milwaukee had high hopes for the future.

CHAPTER 4

BECOMING A SUPERSTAR

Over the next two seasons, Giannis Antetokounmpo just kept getting better. He scored more points. He grabbed more rebounds. He made more **assists**. He blocked more shots. It seemed as if the sky was the limit.

During a 2017 playoff game, the Bucks faced off against the Toronto Raptors.

Antetokounmpo dunks over three Raptors players in a 2017 playoff game.

Antetokounmpo showed off his freakish skills. He went up for a dunk. His right hand hung on to the rim as he slammed the ball through. But his right foot was still touching the ground.

Antetokounmpo scored 28 points in that game. He also had eight rebounds and three assists. The Bucks defeated the Raptors by a score of 97–83.

The Raptors ended up winning the series in six games. But Antetokounmpo was the leading scorer in four of the six games. All around the league, people expected great things from him in the next season. Over the summer, retired NBA star Kobe Bryant even challenged

Antetokounmpo blocks a shot by Raptors guard DeMar DeRozan during a 2017 playoff game.

him to win the Most Valuable Player

(MVP) Award.

Antetokounmpo signed a new contract in 2017. The deal paid him $100 million over four years. He had come a long way since the days in Greece when his family struggled for food.

Antetokounmpo began the 2017–18 season as one of the hottest players in the NBA. Over his first 53 games, he averaged more than 27 points and 10 rebounds. His most spectacular moment came in a game against the New York Knicks. The play started when Bucks small forward Khris Middleton stole the ball and started moving down the court. Antetokounmpo was right behind him. Middleton gently lobbed the ball up.

Bucks fans are getting used to seeing incredible dunks from Antetokounmpo.

Antetokounmpo jumped all the way over a Knicks defender and made a slam dunk!

Bucks fans hoped to celebrate amazing plays like that one for years to come. After all, Giannis Antetokounmpo was one of the brightest young stars in the NBA.

GIANNIS ANTETOKOUNMPO

- Height: 6 feet 11 inches (211 cm)
- Weight: 222 pounds (101 kg)
- Birth date: December 6, 1994
- Birthplace: Athens, Greece
- Club team: Filathlitikos (Athens, Greece) (2012–2013)
- NBA team: Milwaukee Bucks (2013–)
- Major awards: NBA Most Improved Player (2017); NBA All-Star (2017, 2018); NBA All-Rookie Second Team (2014)

Milwaukee

Athens

Lagos

FOCUS ON
GIANNIS ANTETOKOUNMPO

Write your answers on a separate piece of paper.

1. Write a paragraph that summarizes the main idea of Chapter 2.

2. Which of Antetokounmpo's skills do you think caused the Bucks to draft him?

3. Which team defeated the Bucks in the 2017 playoffs?

> **A.** Portland Trail Blazers
> **B.** Toronto Raptors
> **C.** New York Knicks

4. Why did most scouts think Antetokounmpo wouldn't succeed in the NBA?

> **A.** because he grew up in a poor neighborhood
> **B.** because he was not done growing yet
> **C.** because he had never faced good opponents

Answer key on page 32.

GLOSSARY

assists
Passes that lead directly to a teammate scoring a basket.

draft
A system that allows teams to acquire new players coming into a league.

luxuries
Things that are nice to have but not necessary.

playoffs
A set of games played after the regular season to decide which team will be the champion.

rebounds
Plays in which a player controls the ball after a missed shot.

rookie
A professional athlete in his or her first year.

scouts
People whose jobs involve looking for talented young players.

wingspan
The distance from the tip of one hand to the tip of the other hand, when a person stretches out his or her arms.

TO LEARN MORE

BOOKS

Fishman, Jon M. *Giannis Antetokounmpo*. Minneapolis: Lerner Publications, 2019.

Moussavi, Sam. *Milwaukee Bucks*. New York: AV2 by Weigl, 2016.

Whiting, Jim. *Milwaukee Bucks*. Mankato, MN: Creative Education, 2017.

NOTE TO EDUCATORS

Visit **www.focusreaders.com** to find lesson plans, activities, links, and other resources related to this title.

INDEX

Antetokounmpo, Thanasis, 12–13
Athens, Greece, 11

Bryant, Kobe, 24

Chicago Bulls, 21

Europe, 20

Filathlitikos, 14

Greek national team, 20

Hammond, John, 15

Lagos, Nigeria, 11

McCollum, C. J., 6
Middleton, Khris, 26
Milwaukee Bucks, 5–9, 15, 17, 19–21, 23–24, 26–27
Most Valuable Player Award, 25

National Basketball Association, 13–14, 17–19, 24, 26–27
NBA Draft, 15
NBA Summer League, 20
New York Knicks, 26–27

Portland Trail Blazers, 5–7

Toronto Raptors, 23–24

Answer Key: 1. Answers will vary; **2.** Answers will vary; **3.** B; **4.** C